MOUNTAIN GARDEN

MOUNTAIN GARDEN

BY

WILL OTTLEY

Illustrations by Chloë Holt

Perpetualaum Books

Published in 2014 by Perpetualaum Books, 4 Berridge Mews,
London NW6 1RF, United Kingdom

Text copyright © 2013 Will Ottley
Illustrations © 2013 Chloë Holt RCA FRSA

Will Ottley and Chloë Holt have asserted their moral right to be identified
as the author and illustrator of this work

A CIP catalogue record for this book is available from the British Library

ISBN 978-0-9927763-1-2

Cover design by Derek Murphy copyright © 2013 Will Ottley

www.mountaingarden.co.uk
www.chloeholt.co.uk

To Grace

Contents

PROLOGUE

THE WOLVES DESCENDED IN PACKS FROM the grasslands into the beech woods. They attacked, dragging the deer to the ground. Buckan fought them. All the stags fought them, with Buckan's father leading the charge. They drove back the wolves, allowing the does and fawns to flee. The cost was high.

'Run, Buckan, and find the Great King Stag,' said his father. 'Take our two fastest stags and head for the mountain. The King will know what to do. He is our only hope.'

As Buckan galloped into the darkening wood, with two stags at his side, he could hear snarling wolves in pursuit.

Suddenly, three lions stepped out from the trees. A pair of screeching pheasants flapped through the branches and a solitary feather floated to the ground. Buckan gasped and swerved towards his lion allies. At last they had come to help. But something in their eyes alarmed him. A feeling of danger made him cry out a warning. Too late, as swiping claws overwhelmed the other stags.

He raced off alone to find the Great King.

CHAPTER I

BEECH WOODS

BUCKAN GALLOPED THROUGH THE MOONLIT shadows of the beech woods, straining his eyes as he peered into the darkness. The saliva on his muzzle dried as the wind rushed past. He dared not heed his lungs that cried out for him to pull up. He could hear the wolves panting and spluttering. They were no longer baying. Was he slowing down, or were they speeding up? His once agile legs felt weak, and he stumbled over the smallest variance in the ground, tripping on fallen boughs that would not have bothered him before. He began to feel detached from his body, from his straining ribs, floating separately alongside the pumping mass of flesh and bone.

He jarred his fetlock. His mind jolted back to his body and panic drummed through his temples. How much longer could he keep going? An internal darkness overwhelmed him. He thought of the deer fighting for their lives. A fight for the survival of everything he knew, everything he was, everything that was good in him. Strengthening his resolve, he breathed through flared nostrils, and a bolt of fresh energy surged within his limbs. The deer depended on him.

He tumbled over a tree root, and as he tried to recover himself he slipped on the uneven moss and plunged towards the ground. His antlers caught the soil, pitching earth and moss into his eyes. His head yanked to one side as his body slewed through the undergrowth. He jumped up, shaking his antlers free. It was too late.

A snarling wolf leapt at him, muscled jaws snapping at his shoulder. Buckan cried out – more from the shock of physical contact than from the pain that shot down his leg. He swung his head around, catching the wolf with antler bone. The wolf squealed and fell back into the darkness.

Two more wolves sprang forward, slobber dripping from their mouths. Moonlight glinted on their incisors. He charged them, butting one into the air. The other, powerfully built with a sloping back, slipped to the side and leapt at him, knocking him off balance. He staggered under the wolf's weight, but he knew not to fall. The wolf tugged on Buckan's neck. Panic strangled a cry. Twisting quickly, he threw the wolf from his back, swiping him with his antlers. The wolf's wild bloodshot eyes shone with terror. The air rasped in Buckan's lungs. He couldn't last much longer. Turning away from his fallen foe, he bolted through the trees.

He hurried on through the blue darkness, crossed by shafts of moonlight. He thought he heard sounds, but each time he turned to check there was only silence punctuated by his own breath. Confused, he darted forward. Or did he simply walk and stumble? He could not remember, but at some point he was standing still in the darkness, licking his dry lips, his mind consumed with the wolves, lions and deer. In the silence, the still beech trees seemed to threaten him. As he took a step forward he was shaking and could barely stand. His head hung low to the ground. How long had he been standing like this? His white forelimbs were streaked in black lines that shone dark red in the moonlight. Falling to his knees, he became aware of tears dripping down his face. He had to rest.

It was the dream that had haunted Buckan since he

was a fawn: a double rainbow. He ran with his sister through the damp grass towards the curving colours in the sky. Then, he saw his sister's lifeless body floating in a stream and the killer's dark eyes staring from the far bank. The unblinking eyes seemed to pin Buckan to the spot. He felt sick, mesmerised by them. The eyes vanished and he became aware of his mother's voice calling.

He awoke with the familiar tightness in his throat, the old feeling of helplessness and guilt disorientating him. Registering beech trees, he tried to recall where he was, before the sharp realisation: he had awoken from one nightmare into another.

His aching body juddered as lightning flashed in the clouds above him, illuminating the woods. Thunder cleaved the darkness, shaking the ground, and the branches swayed. Rain spattered the leaves, and broke onto his fur. He lay in the wet and cold foreboding air, feeling the warmth of his own body against the soil. Numbness gave way to a single pervading thought: what if he failed? He heard a deep sigh and realised that it had come from his own throat. He nuzzled into the leaves and drifted back into uneasy sleep.

In his dreams he was a young fawn again, alone by the river. His body shivered as an orb of white light approached him from the water. He heard his sister's voice: *'When darkness falls the White Stag will gather the forces of light.'*

CHAPTER II

GREAT KING STAG

BUCKAN KEPT TO THE BACK PATHS LEADING towards the snow-capped mountain. He started at the slightest sound. The birds flying up from the undergrowth set his heart racing. Feeling stiff at first, he hobbled a little. As his body gently stretched, it regained strength and his movement eased. Little cobwebs on the ground and in the trees shone in the morning light. All around glistened a world of symmetry. He breathed the moist air and his connection with the woods returned, a reassuring resonance that he had sensed since a fawn. These strong trees were his friends, no matter where he was heading.

When the white peak became obscured by beech trees, he followed the stream uphill. He stopped to drink where the waters of the stream formed a pool. His reflection shocked him. His white coat was muddy and bloodstained, his once glistening eyes red and bleary. He took a gulp of water and then froze. His ears twitched as they detected something – was it a sound or just a feeling?

He was about to dismiss his fear when he heard a branch snap. Something was stalking him. He bounded off through the midday shadows and a clearing appeared beyond a large fallen tree. He gathered all his strength, and leapt.

The sunlight blinded him as he hit the ground. He pulled to a halt, sensing the presence of a powerful being. He swung his gaze to the left, and his face softened as he beheld a great white stag. Tall and rooted to the earth, the majestic beast had a countenance more splendid than he could have ever imagined, and a rare white coat, similar to his own.

'There you are,' said the great stag.

'You were expecting me?' Buckan fell to his knees, his heart beating against his ribcage.

He felt profound relief as he stared into the great stag's steady blue eyes. There was something about them that took his fear away. It was as if he could relax in the presence of true strength.

'Yes, for longer than you may imagine,' said the great stag. He walked over to Buckan, his eyes blazing with energy and warmth. 'Dark forces are pursuing you. Our time is precious.'

The words were softly spoken, but Buckan sensed urgency behind them. It seemed to contradict the great stag's calm demeanour. No, it was not quite that, he thought. The stag was both alert and perfectly contained.

'With more time, I could prepare you for the journey ahead, but the fear would remain. You have been tested already, my friend, but your greatest challenges lie ahead. You must journey on from here, through the Dark Forest to Mountain Garden.'

'Mountain Garden?' The words stumbled from Buckan's mouth. Mountain Garden was a magical place that he had heard mentioned in the fairy tales of his fawnhood. As he searched the great stag's eyes for understanding, he gasped at the air. 'But we need to overcome the vicious wolves that are invading our land. The deer have been fighting them for days. The old alliance with the lions is broken. More wolf packs are crossing the lion grasslands and pouring into the beech woods. We need to gather a great army.'

'Be calm, my friend. Sometimes it is better to

withdraw before you advance. You must win the battle before you fight. Go to Mountain Garden and embrace the power that awaits you there. You need to undertake this test alone, for only then can you hope to defeat the enemy.'

Buckan rose from his knees. He looked down at the great stag's shadow, unsure how to proceed.

'I heed what you say. I heard about Mountain Garden in the tales of my youth. They say it lies hidden at the summit of the white-topped mountain.'

'In a sense it is hidden, but you can go there directly. Find out for yourself, then there's no doubt.'

The great stag turned away to face the edge of the clearing. 'Time is slipping away, my friend. Listen to your instinct and those beings of highest resonance. Take courage. No matter what adversities you meet, keep going with a strong heart.'

A lion's roar tore through the clearing. A huge beast emerged from the trees, his dark red mane caressing the scars criss-crossing his body. The great stag faced him. The lion paused.

'We meet again, Lion. I see that anger is still consuming you.'

'I've come to regain my rightful place, Great King Stag,' roared Lion.

The Great King Stag glanced at Buckan. 'Things are not always as they seem,' he said. 'Love dissolves fear.'

Buckan was shaking uncontrollably but, fighting the urge to flee, he took assurance from the Great King Stag's dignified strength. There was no fright at all in his gallant face, unexpectedly full of love and compassion. His ancient body seemed to be glowing. He was closing his eyes, as if to contain an immense energy within.

Buckan felt calmer now. His mind sharpened, his aching body relaxed and, in awe, he watched the scene unfolding before him. The light in the clearing became very bright. Each breath he took stretched out and made him feel as if he were connected to everything.

The clearing lit up as a shimmering golden deer jumped out from the Great King Stag's body. Leaping upwards, the deer rose towards the heavens. Buckan heard, 'My brave friend, follow your heart with love and valour.'

Lion sprang at the Great King Stag, and sank his

teeth into his neck. Yet the Great King Stag offered no resistance, for the spirit had already left his body. Lion paused, looking up into the sky transfixed, his ears twitching.

CHAPTER III

DARK FOREST

BUCKAN CAREERED TOWARDS THE DARK forest, crashing through branches. His antlers ripped away their leaves. His thoughts raced with panic and grief. The deer's great hope was gone. Why hadn't the Great King Stag fought Lion? The magnificent stag was clearly the stronger. He raced on, oblivious to where he was heading, thinking about the threat from the wolves – social animals that had become warmongers. Galloping deeper into the obscure trees, he wanted to leave the danger behind him, feeling that distance might diminish his mental pain. The only thing he knew for certain was that the Great King Stag had told him to find Mountain Garden. There was no other plan.

He was lost, wandering through thickening undergrowth. The ancient trees were now close around him, generating a feeling of mysteriousness, as if rooted to something inexplicable and primal. The vibrancy of these sage-like pillars of furrowed bark was a reassuring connection in the unknown. He was calmer now as he walked onwards, finding little trails and pathways that slowly led him uphill. He could hear occasional birds chattering in the canopy above him, but mostly he walked in silence, winding his way around half-buried boulders and fallen trees.

The terrain had become tougher as the track sloped upwards. Loose rocks now shifted under his hooves. He knocked a rock from the path, and watched it roll against a rotting toadstool with a cadmium orange body, causing tiny flies to swarm up from its putrefying surface. Thorny bramble bushes scratched his skin and tested his patience.

The leaves in the trees languished against a deep crimson sky, its shades varying in the fading light. He looked for a secluded place to rest and chanced upon a narrow trail that deviated slightly from the direction in which he was heading but seemed less steep. He decided to take this easier route and followed the new trail until he came upon a crescent-shaped chestnut tree.

His limbs now trembled with fatigue as he lay down

concealed in bracken. His reassuring connection with the trees was gone. The branches appeared to move towards him. What was that rustling? Was it just the wind? Shivering, he hunched lower under the leaves. He recalled the day's events and felt overwhelmed by unbearable sadness. A faint aroma of sweet flowers wafted through the darkness, consoling him. His thoughts, knotted like ivy, began to untangle.

The lamenting of birds, a confusion of sound, brought him into the day. He stood slowly, looking in the direction of the dawn, and noticed a small cut on his hind leg. He dismissed it. Some white blossom reflected the morning light. His tight brow softened a little.

He resumed his journey, dragging his feet. The track, which undulated and meandered through the trees, was well trodden, and there were plenty of succulent fern shoots to eat and fresh streams to drink from.

Yet the air was humid and time dragged as he followed the winding path. Passing a bush with scarlet blossoms, he found the flowers had no scent at all. After many hours, he was exhausted. When the sun created long shadows around him he decided to rest. He felt as if he was being watched.

In the early evening light, he awoke to find a small brown bat hovering over his hind leg. Two beady eyes squinted at him from a flat face.

'What do you want?' asked Buckan.

'I flew down to check how you were as I noticed you bleeding.' The bat's pink ears and nose twitched.

His haunch was indeed bleeding again. 'It's only a scratch from the brambles. How long have you been watching me?'

'I've just arrived. I'm pleased to make your acquaintance, for this is a lonely place, full of ghosts doing the same things over and over.'

Buckan continued, 'Can you tell me if this path leads to Mountain Garden?'

'Mountain Garden? Ah, yes it does. This is the most direct route,' said Bat, his eyes flitting from tree to tree. 'I know they're tempting, but don't eat the maroon berries on that shiny bush over there. They're poisonous. Even the honey from its pollen is toxic. Now, if you'll excuse me, I have to sleep.' Bat fluttered away into the trees.

Buckan picked up his heavy limbs, his mind intoxicated by drowsiness. He started to walk on down the trail. Having covered little distance, he lay down once more. He dreamed about a small stream flowing into a golden garden with sunflowers flanked by ancient oak trees. Surely this was Mountain Garden? But as he walked towards it, the garden receded, and the faster he went, the faster it receded.

His eyes sprang open, sensing danger. He caught sight of Bat sucking at his hind leg, his sharp front teeth covered in blood.

Buckan jumped up, startling Bat, who scurried away along the ground on his winged forelimbs until Buckan trapped him under his hoof.

'So it's you who has been causing my leg to bleed and sapping my strength while I slept. Pretending to help me while feeding off me!'

'It's not my fault that everyone feeds off each other. I was only taking a little drop of blood to stay alive in this cruel world.'

'You would feed off me until my own powers were spent and my chances lost, you trickster! Preying on others when you could choose to fly high instead.'

Buckan let Bat fly away, feeling as if he had woken from a dream. In front of him was the crescent-shaped chestnut tree again. He must have travelled in a circle.

CHAPTER IV

SWAMP

THE DENSE CANOPY OBSCURED THE LIGHT as Buckan walked beneath it. Moist ivy brushed against his face, and his nostrils filled with the dank smell of fungi. He stepped over branches, knowing that any sound would alert his enemies. His head was aching, and pressure pulsed behind his tired eyes as he picked a way through the trees. He was far from the beech woods of home.

He came to a clearing and cantered through lush green grass in the crisp morning breeze. The warm sunlight on his back lifted his spirits. A light breeze brought with it the smell of pine from the direction of the distant mountain. Passing a solitary white crocus, he entered a glade of copper beech trees. He belonged amongst these elegant trees. It was such a familiar sight that for a moment the threat from the wolves seemed all but gone. The oscillating leaves emanated calmness.

A light mist thickened into a grey fog and he paused, his ears flicking backwards and forwards to detect possible dangers. The atmosphere unsettled him. Was it the absence of birds? There was a nauseating smell of decay. His hooves squelched into fetid grass and stagnant water. A wide channel blocked his path. As he prepared himself to cross it, his mouth went dry and his shoulders stiffened. Feeling queasy, he knew he must cross quickly or he would fail to cross at all.

He waded through the filthy water, the mud sucking at his hooves. His heart pounded as he heard splashes. He leapt for the far bank, reached it in two bounds and stepped into the trees.

'Can you help me?' said a frail voice behind him.

Turning, the contour of a submerged head stared at him from the water's edge.

'What's wrong?'

'My foot is lodged under this fallen bough.'

Buckan edged closer to the bank. A flock of honking geese flew overhead in a V formation high above the trees.

It was too murky to see the creature's face, which was partly obscured by leaves. The eyes were narrow, bulging and dark, but Buckan couldn't detect malice. In fact he couldn't detect much at all, only a blank gaze that went straight through him.

'I came to your aid just moments ago,' the creature continued. 'I stopped a water snake from striking you, and that's how I trapped my foot. I can give you directions to Mountain Garden, if that's your destination.'

'You know of Mountain Garden?' asked Buckan.

'Yes. Now please help me.'

Keeping a cautious distance between himself and the unblinking eyes, Buckan placed his antlers against the fallen bough, and pushed hard.

Suddenly the eyes became a gaping jaw with fierce yellow teeth as Crocodile leapt at him, his powerful tail propelling his huge scaly bulk forward.

Buckan tried to jump away, lowering his antlers, but Crocodile seized them in his teeth. Buckan lurched backwards to free himself but he was held fast. Crocodile thrashed about, twisting, pulling him off balance, and dragging him into the quagmire.

Sweat poured into Buckan's eyes and his body shook with effort. He felt nauseous, as if a dark energy

were sapping his strength. But he refused to give up. Several times he pulled Crocodile back from the water, but then he would lose ground, his hooves sliding further into the mud. Crocodile's dead weight wore him down. Muddy water splashed his face. He felt a surge of anger. How could he have fallen for such a simple trick? The harder he tried to escape Crocodile's jaws, the more he was drawn into the mire.

'Give up, young buck,' said Crocodile, through clenched teeth and foul breath. 'Give up your struggle for life. You're mine, like all the others.'

Crocodile pulled Buckan's head down into the water. Buckan held his breath for as long as he could, while the strength seeped from his exhausted body.

His mind began to cloud over with flashing pictures from his past: his fawnhood tree, long walks with his mother. He recalled the wolves coming into the beech woods, then the Great King Stag stood before him in the clearing, speaking to him.

'True strength comes from connecting to the source of love, Buckan, not just from the power of your muscles. Release your delusion of separation and free yourself from this crocodile.'

'But Crocodile is holding me down.'

'Not so, it is you who is holding the crocodile.'

The Great King Stag's words shocked Buckan and gave him new strength. He raised his head effortlessly from the water. Gasping for breath, he savoured the power returning to his limbs. Looking down, he glimpsed his own reflection – an imposing white stag. Joy lit up his heart as, one step after another, he pulled the crocodile from the swamp. The stubborn creature held onto him with increasing force, but with a simple twist of his head, Buckan broke free from the heinous jaws.

Crocodile stared at him, confusion in his eyes.

'So it is you,' he said, 'still looking for a fairy-tale garden.'

'We've not met before, and it seems you know nothing of Mountain Garden.'

'My memory is not so poor, Great King Stag. You think you can defeat me this time, rather than jumping over me?'

Just as Buckan realised Crocodile's confusion in thinking him the Great King Stag, the reptile charged him with open jaws. Buckan lowered his head and stepped forward to counter the impact, his antler piercing Crocodile's eye. The armoured hulk slammed to the ground twitching, chest heaving. Standing over him, Buckan cast his gaze downwards as the last breath left Crocodile's body.

CHAPTER V

Mountain Pass

THE FOREST WAS BECOMING THINNER WITH altitude. Strong sunlight streamed through the open treetops. Evergreens with spiky needles had replaced the broadleaf trees, and the smell of pine filled Buckan's nostrils. As he cantered uphill, the physical effort brought unexpected solace. He felt a deftness that removed the fatigue. He reached a ford in a fast-flowing river and checked carefully for danger, twitching his ears and glancing around. He was about to cross, when a large salmon jumped out of the water, startling him.

'Oh, sorry,' said Salmon. 'Sometimes I have to leap over things to keep to the main channel.'

'How do you know which way to go?'

'Instinct!' Salmon said. 'Actually, it's the current against my scales. If I can't swim, I'll jump. If the rock looks too big, I'll wait... Once I came across a large wall that blocked my path. I knew there must be a way through but I couldn't see it. Then a cloud shifted and

the wall was gone. It was just a play of light.' Salmon headed triumphantly on upriver.

Buckan smiled as he crossed the river. Although the rocky path sloped down almost as much as up, he was gaining altitude.

The sun disappeared behind a ridge, its light bending into distinct beams before the sky turned a silvery pink. Plumes of Buckan's breath froze in the crisp air as he searched for a sheltered place to rest. He knew the evening would be bitterly cold on an exposed mountain pass. Finding a copse of fir trees, he lay down in some thick mountain fern to keep warm and drifted into a peaceful sleep.

He saw a figure standing on a faraway rock, an exquisite golden feminine form. He admired her long graceful limbs and large clear eyes in the moonlight: a golden doe. Her slender head turned towards him. In her gentle gaze he felt a tender sensation in his heart. She smiled. His heart was filled with an immense joy, acceptance and love. Buckan wanted to approach her, to be with her, when a movement behind distracted him. He turned just in time to glimpse a shadow slipping away into the bushes. His muscles tightened in fear.

He opened his eyes to the sound of the wind whispering through the trees, stirring him to recall where he was and why. An aching void in his stomach urged him to forget the wind's cry, to roll over and obliterate the world from his mind. No physical nourishment could quench this emptiness. The dark shadow of his dream gripped him in a torment, smothering his enthusiasm in melancholic fog. But as he remembered the Golden Doe, his clenched jaw relaxed a little. He took a deep breath and stood up: he had to keep going.

Buckan walked from the line of trees onto a path that led straight up the mountain. The narrow track hugged the rock on one side, with a steep drop to a river valley on the other. A headwind was blowing into Buckan's face, forming ice on the sharp edges around him. His ribs quivered as he tried to avoid slipping. He began to panic: rocks were rolling away from under his hooves, falling down the mountainside and taking other rocks in their wake. The wind brought rain, which turned to sleet and snow. Buckan's strength was tested as he battled against the storm. By the early evening he could barely move his aching legs. Bowing his head, keeping close to the side of the mountain, he tentatively checked each foothold before committing his full weight. Was he even close to Mountain Garden?

With blurred eyes he peered through the thickening snow and fading light. As the cold bit into him he stumbled, falling onto his haunches. Desperate for rest and exposed on the path, he hauled himself up to take another step. He noticed a warm white light reflected by the snow. Could it be moonlight? Raising his gaze, he beheld the Golden Doe standing in front of him. In her graceful presence his body eased and his heart relaxed. He was now oblivious to the storm, and felt only her radiant love. Exhausted, he lay down against the rock, insulated in a bed of snow.

Buckan pictured a long corridor of trees, mighty oaks with large limbs stretching high above him. The brilliant sun permeating the leaves bathed him in green iridescent light. The lush grass was sprinkled with wild orchids in many colours: indigo, vermilion, amber and white. He breathed in the soothing aroma of jasmine bushes and heard the gentle sound of a waterfall. He became aware that each blade of grass, leaf and branch was vibrating to the resounding water. The multiple colours and planes seemed to merge into one.

Statues of stag warriors stood between the shimmering trees. As Buckan walked slowly down the long corridor, each proud warrior stirred ancient memories in him. Then an acceptance: of the light, the not-so-light, and even the darkness that lay deep inside him. He walked to a giant copper beech with a trunk so wide that he could not guess its age. Beyond it, a river pool was gleaming in the leafy sunlight. He plunged into its deep crystal-clear waters and waves of possibility enveloped him.

The rising sun gleamed at Buckan from the distant horizon and a single shaft of light fell onto his face. With the cold air in his nostrils, his muscles felt tight but surprisingly warm in the bed of snow. He was tucked inside a rock hollow. The storm, long since passed, had been replaced by stillness. He lay a while to ponder his vision from the previous night, before standing. To his amazement, where the Golden Doe had stood was a sheer drop. The path had fallen away.

He retraced his steps with new energy. He looked with fresh appreciation at the sun-tipped mountain peaks, the rays of morning light glinting on the icy slopes. Down below in the lush green river valley, a haze was forming over the trees. How many times would he gaze at such a scene? The sun was rising.

CHAPTER VI

HIGH PASS

BUCKAN CAME TO A FORK IN THE TRAIL THAT he had missed the previous night. He took a new path splitting off at a higher elevation. He heard a pair of eagles issuing a call, rising on the circular currents above the valley. It was as if nothing existed but him, the eagles, and the mountain.

In places, falling rocks had eroded the narrow pass. As he picked a way across the precarious scree, he heard a high-pitched crack and only just avoided some large boulders racing past him.

He ran, twisting his body to avoid the crashing rocks, until he reached firm ground. His heart was still thumping when the sun came out from behind a cloud and bathed him in its warmth, as if to celebrate this small moment of courage.

He squinted at the snow-covered slopes above him. He saw little footprints leading to a small rock hollow. The rippled shadows in the windswept snow

accentuated the deep blue sky. There was no protection from the elements up here. Beauty and danger entwined in a spirited dance.

As he rounded a rocky outcrop, a bearded brown mountain goat with short sturdy legs blocked his path. His broad head supported large knobbly horns that curved upwards over a muscled body, while his hazel eyes, which held Buckan's gaze, barely seemed to conceal anger.

'Hello, Mountain Goat.'

'I'm no mountain goat,' said the creature, rising to his full stature. 'I'm Steinbock the Mountain King. I've been watching you trespass across our pathways. You are quite lost. This land belongs to the Steinbocks, forest dweller, and you must turn back.'

'Noble Steinbock, my homeland, the beech woods, is under attack from wolves,' said Buckan, bewildered by the creature's cold manner. 'I seek only a safe passage to Mountain Garden.'

'The altitude has affected your judgement if you seek a garden amongst this ice and snow. Don't you think I would know if there were a garden on this mountain? Your delusion is matched only by your arrogance to venture up here. I've beaten many challengers over the years. Leave now or face the consequences. Unless you think it's honourable to die in battle?'

'But what a senseless battle this would be!'

'I see you leave me no choice,' said Steinbock, rearing up on his hind legs to knock Buckan off the path.

Buckan retreated several steps as Steinbock charged. The clash of their horns echoed around the rocky crags. While their torsos were locked together, their hooves slid over the icy gravel, perilously close to the edge of the path.

On the mountain, Steinbock's shorter stature seemed to have the advantage over Buckan's tall frame. They stood, heaving against each other. Steam filled the air around their nostrils. The cold mountain wind whistled over the jagged cliff and chilled the sweat on their struggling bodies. As Buckan fought Steinbock's unrelenting attempts to throw him off the path, he felt the energy draining away from his aching limbs.

'You seek to belittle me, White Stag?' Steinbock snorted, breaking off the attack and shaking his body.

Buckan was too tired to speak. He gasped for breath

as Steinbock hurtled forward once more. They collided again and Buckan was disorientated, feeling a trickle of blood running down the side of his head. He lost his footing. Was the path beginning to crumble beneath them? Steinbock scrambled onto solid ground. The path continued to fall away from Buckan with a crash of sliding rocks. He was fighting to cling on, dust clouds biting his eyes. He was falling.

When the dust settled, Buckan was gripping with his front legs, his hind legs hanging in the air. Steinbock's strong horns, locked in his antlers, were all that prevented Buckan from falling. With just one twist of his head, Steinbock could send him to his death, hundreds of feet below. Buckan's exhausted body trembled. He closed his eyes. He had failed to reach Mountain Garden. He had not just let down the deer: he had failed himself. A tear ran down his dusty face at this realisation.

Steinbock reared, tossing Buckan into the air. Buckan hit the path behind him, wincing, and opened his eyes as the confusion in his mind cleared. Was he still alive? He rolled away from the cliff edge and scrabbled to his feet. Steinbock had gone. A sound of stones rolling above caught his attention. Glancing up, he saw Steinbock striding across an impossibly steep rock face and disappearing into the distance.

CHAPTER VII

CAVE

BUCKAN WALKED ALONG THE HIGH PASS, edging with difficulty through the fresh deep snow. Ahead of him, he could see a black-and-white jagged peak jutting up into the silver sky. He hesitated before a vast expanse that sloped down towards a precipice. Surely there must be an easier crossing place? The mountain above was a sheer wall of ice. His eyes scanned its surface, up through the clouds, and rested upon the barbed peak with spindrift blowing from its sharp summit.

He agonised over whether to cross in the fading light but silenced his doubts and slipped into soft white powder up to his haunches. The going was even harder than he'd expected. His hooves pushed through a hidden crust and unbalanced him. The ground shook and a torrent of icy cold air hit his body. Snow cascaded down the slope, rolling him over and over. Engulfed in snow, he tumbled down the mountainside and fell through layers of ice into a deep crevasse. The crashing of the ice drowned his cries. He slammed onto his right side, unable to move. More snow piled on top of him, pressing his lungs. Desperate for air, he fought to clear his mouth and nostrils. The avalanche sealed the opening far above, shutting him into silence. He raised his head in panic, and groaned at a shooting pain in his right haunch. He blacked out, overcome in the icy darkness.

The sound of flowing water far below brought him back to awareness. The fear returned as he sensed a vibration – was it the ground moving or his own body shaking with exhaustion? A shaft of light from above shone onto the ledge. He tried to turn aside, but his right hind leg was limp and a biting pain shot through his spine. A sharp rock poked into his ribs, and he forced it away. It rolled, then a splash of deep water in the far distance echoed off the walls. The hair on his back stood on end. He shut his eyes and slowly opened them again as a feeling of aloneness overtook him.

Buckan lay still. Mind failing him, he could not reason a way out. Thoughts returned to the beech woods of home, recalling the savage wolves, his father's anguished face and the lions' betrayal. He felt trapped, consumed by these bleak mental clouds. The only relief was the shaft of fading light and the promise of sleep.

He was woken again by bright sunlight. It reflected off the azure ice, beaming a spectrum of colours onto his eyelids. He could see marbled columns rising around him, a cathedral to the might of nature. He felt his own minuscule stature. His insignificance was underlined by the sharp angles and fault lines, which seemed to have been twisted by extraordinary forces.

As he lay in silence, drifting in and out of consciousness, he saw her again: the Golden Doe stood close beside him. Their eyes met. Through her gaze he felt boundless warmth flowing within his heart and running through the cells of his body. Love emanated from her, filling him with new hope. She turned and walked away through the cave wall.

His mind basked in the undisturbed stillness. All that remained was his breath, an infinite calmness and the colours of light merging into a single point. He was in perfect harmony with these mountains. He was part of them. Their strength was his strength. His fear dissolved and his heart filled with peace and joy.

Buckan rolled off the ledge and fell into the abyss. He slammed into the water below and felt a sharp jolt in his injured leg. As he swam up to the surface, the icy water numbed the pain. He found he could move his leg once more. A strong current carried him to the far wall of the cavern. He was sucked down by the swirling torrent and carried into a subterranean channel. The water propelled him beneath the rock.

Just when he felt he could no longer hold his breath, a powerful force expelled him up to the surface of an underground river. He gasped for air, overjoyed to be alive. Then he heard the crashing of a waterfall and realised he was going over the edge of the mountain.

The deafening water gushed around him as he tumbled towards a deep pool at the bottom of the waterfall. His body twisted and turned as vicious currents pulled at him, holding him down. Breaking free, he glided to the surface of the foam. He swam to the riverbank with the last of his strength and staggered onto dry land. Exhausted, he lay down on a patch of soft grass. Slowly his blurred vision began to focus. A beautiful garden lay before him.

CHAPTER VIII

MOUNTAIN GARDEN

A GENTLE MIST WAS DRIFTING TOWARDS THE large meadow, refracting the shimmering light. Buckan was eager to explore. He stepped through soft grass, covered in radiant flowers: wild orchids of amethyst and ultramarine, purple lavender and glossy jasmine bushes with pearl-white blossom. He breathed the essence of mountain flowers, a medley of sweet aromas, and the scent of pine. Ancient copper beech trees, oaks and firs flanked the meadow, their strong broad limbs resplendent with different shades of emerald and copper foliage. Their roots were ablaze with electric violet and citron blossoms. Against the backdrop of the mountain, the crashing waterfall boomed a deep primal sound. With every moment Buckan felt more at peace and more energised. The garden seemed familiar to him.

'Hello, Buckan. I've been waiting for you.'

'You have?' said Buckan, looking for the source of

the voice. He was startled to see a black stallion with piercing amber eyes and a long gleaming mane.

'May I ask how you know me?'

'I'm your gardener and this is your garden.'

'My garden?' said Buckan. 'But I haven't been here before.'

'Don't you recognise this place? You've planted many beautiful ideas in this garden, removing weeds and much dead wood.'

'I have? It feels so uplifting here, after that freezing mountain.'

'You have opened your heart, and the cold storms of fear and doubt have subsided. Welcome to Mountain Garden, Buckan. You are ready to realise your destiny.'

As Buckan contemplated Stallion's strong words and presence, his eyes lingered on a songbird swooping down towards an ancient oak. White light emanated from the edges of the bushy evergreen leaves. Looking down, he was amazed to see the same white light around his own hooves.

'Can the energy of Mountain Garden help us defend ourselves against the wolves and lions?'

'It will be challenging, Buckan. A dark force has emerged from the shadows. Fear is limiting; it destroys life and beauty. In hatred the wolves have forgotten their true nature and become vulnerable. When you connect to Mountain Garden you remain strongly rooted in love. This will overcome fear.'

Looking across the meadow, beyond a row of bright purple foxgloves, Buckan noticed a scorched oak tree split in two.

'You faced your deepest fears on that mountain,' said Stallion, following Buckan's gaze. 'Whenever you wavered in your faith, violent storms and lightning hit this garden.'

Buckan walked across the meadow, frowning at the sight of the stricken oak. He took a sharp breath, as beyond it an entire valley of trees was blackened by fire. Large trunks lay on the ground, some still smouldering. A few of the taller trees, though scorched at the base, maintained their green canopy. The sunlight streamed through their leaves onto the ground.

'At times, I worried this garden might be completely consumed by fire,' said Stallion. 'The spray from the waterfall saved this precious area, and look, there are green shoots coming through that were not there yesterday. Emptiness brings rapid change.'

Buckan was silent, fighting back the tears that welled up in his eyes.

'It was so hard, I didn't think I would make it,' he said at last. 'But I had help, both from the Great King Stag and from the beautiful Golden Doe.'

'A goddess, the embodiment of tenderness and compassion,' said Stallion.

'I wish I could meet her in a living form.'

'With grace, you will meet her,' said Stallion, 'although by nature, flesh and blood is different from a goddess.'

Buckan looked back over his arduous journey across the mountain, and remembered how the Golden Doe, with her loving energy, had helped him. He sighed, turning away in silence to watch the sun descending in the carmine sky, a golden sphere with a hue of fire. The garden was resplendent in the twilight.

'I must rest. Tomorrow I will explore the garden fully.'

'You must leave at dawn, Buckan. Every moment is precious.'

'I must leave? I have only just arrived.'

'Do you see those dark clouds on the horizon? You must face what has caused this destruction.'

'But I don't want to go. I want to stay and embrace the strength of this magical place.'

'The loving source is unlimited, Buckan, and is not confined to this garden. It's within you. You can progress swiftly, as many obstacles have been removed.'

Buckan raised his gaze. He walked through the long grass, deep in thought, looking in awe at the waterfall that had brought him here. He lay down in sweet-smelling lavender bushes and closed his eyes. His mind relaxed, absorbing the soothing sound of the waterfall. An eyelid closed very softly in his mind.

An orb of light floated towards him in his dream, 'We are loved,' said his sister's voice. '*We are love.*' The orb faded and a wild rose remained in her place.

At dawn he stood up slowly to feast his eyes on the flowers and trees around him, feeling supreme bliss as he stretched his limbs. Two songbirds were harmonising joyfully. He walked over to Stallion, who was standing beneath a copper beech, his presence

loving and reassuring.

'I must depart, my dear friend.'

'You must, but remember, you can return in an instant. Keep the power of this garden alive in your heart: the sound and vibration of the waterfall, your breath, the subtle light in the trees.'

CHAPTER IX

River

BUCKAN WALKED BESIDE THE CRYSTALLINE river that flowed from the waterfall. Gazing back at Mountain Garden, he felt a strong urge to remain. The garden had enthralled him, filling him with love for everything – the rocks, the trees, the birds and his own existence. Glancing across the river, he saw Salmon was swimming towards him.

'We meet again,' said Buckan.

'Hello, my friend. I have reached Mountain Falls, the source of the river. I was born here, and so I travelled across the ocean to return home to this precious place once more.'

'Was the journey worthwhile?'

'Yes, because as I look back, every curve in the river, every current in the ocean, finally makes perfect sense. When I left this mountain as a young salmon I was unsettled and headstrong. I wanted to experience the world to find happiness and love. I've had many experiences, some good and some less so. There are plenty of predators in that deep sea. I became lost and despondent. Then I began to realise that my outer world reflected my inner thinking, and that the true answers actually lay inside me. What a revelation that was! I overcame my fears and frustrations internally and they vanished externally. I learned that the love we give comes back to us.'

Buckan smiled. 'So long, my wise friend, and thank you.'

The passage down the river was effortless. Buckan felt as if he was walking through the beech woods of old, with white light pervading every space. For the first time in his journey, time was on his side.

He followed the sparkling water downstream. The sunlight reflected off its fast-flowing surface, and its subtle currents played a sweet melody. In places the main channel was joined by tempestuous rocky tributaries, which Buckan easily crossed by jumping from boulder to boulder, avoiding the trees that appeared to grow out of the rocks themselves.

Buckan saw the remains of a large tree floating towards him. Its giant scorched roots looked as if they had been torn from the earth. It brushed the side of the bank. He stepped onto it without thinking, and was carried along the watercourse. He stood on its broad trunk, floating through winding valleys and into the lower regions of the mountain. At times the river narrowed, and as the water squeezed through rocky channels it became rougher. But the sheer mass of the tree and its large outstretched boughs kept it stable in the water.

He floated past a red squirrel that was standing on the bank, sobbing.

'What saddens you?' he asked, but the squirrel seemed not to notice him.

At the bottom of the mountain, he was carried right through the Dark Forest towards the beech woods. The river channel was wider now, and ran deep and fast.

As Buckan neared the far edge of the forest, something was unsettling him. He began to feel stifled, and stared transfixed at the riverbank. The white light around the trees had been replaced by greyness. He noticed the grass moving on the bank. Something was tracking him. A pair of sharp black eyes suddenly flashed. He tried to cry out but no sound came. His pulse thundered against his temples while he struggled to keep his balance. Panic was overpowering him and he stumbled from the tree. His hindquarters splashed into the icy water. His head thumped against the thick bark and his mouth filled with water. What a fool he had been to think a pretty garden could save him or the deer!

In his mind's eye, lightning flashed in Mountain Garden and somewhere inside him Stallion's gentle voice was speaking, calming him. 'Can you hear the sound of the waterfall, Buckan? Love dissolves all fear.'

'I know what happened to me as I fell,' he realised, now aware of the icy water. He pulled himself once more onto the trunk, using the branches. The light returned to the trees.

The river meandered through tree-lined valleys. The floating trunk carried Buckan towards a large granite dome at the edge of the thinning forest. Its top was shrouded in mist. Staring at it, his instinct told him to leave the river but for a moment he was doubtful: he was close to home and the beech woods. The thought of returning to the riverbank made him uncomfortable. But trusting his instincts, he jumped into the icy water.

He swam with the current to the bank, noticing a steep narrow path running up the side of the mount that towered above him. He left the water and began to climb the vibrant rock, feeling stronger as the mist parted to reveal a golden evening sun.

CHAPTER X

Granite Dome

A S HE REACHED THE SUMMIT, BUCKAN WAS challenged by two mighty stags. Their stern gaze and bloodshot eyes softened at the sight of him.

'Young Lord,' said one, 'we have been awaiting your arrival.'

'My friends, I have come to help you fight the wolves, but I didn't know that I was expected.'

'Sir, the Great King Stag said that in the darkest hour we must come to this mount and await the White Stag. He told us that sinister forces would descend when he was gone and that a great white stag would take his place. There can be no doubt that you have fulfilled the prophecy.'

'The Great King Stag had insight,' said Buckan with a shiver.

Buckan's father cantered forward to greet him. As he raised himself up, his tired grey eyes shone with joy.

'Buckan, I scarcely recognise you. I hardly dared

hope that you would return safely. I see a power in you that I have only perceived in the Great King Stag. You have become a true warrior and I am proud of you.'

Tears welled up in Buckan's eyes. His father deserved such affection: his honourable presence was strong and wise. Buckan felt thankful to have completed the task.

'Father, I have missed you, Mother, and all the deer. I have travelled far to Mountain Garden on the instructions of the Great King Stag. I know I have changed, and I only hope it is enough. Now please tell me what has happened since I left you in the beech woods.'

'When you left the battle, your mother led the fawns and the older deer to the hidden plateau, using our strong stags and does to protect them from the wolves. They remain there in hiding. The wolves attacked us, and the treacherous lions mauled us and drove us back. We were able to draw them away from the plateau with our counterattacks. We fought hard, and at times it looked as if we would prevail, but there were simply too many of them and our brave stags fell one by one. Then we heard that the Great King Stag had been killed in battle with King Lion. Our scouts witnessed Lion standing over the Great King Stag's lifeless body. We joined with the Great King's forces to make our way to this rock. I fear that this will be our last stand. Our position is strong, but the combined forces of the wolves and the lions are deadly.'

'Father, I was with the Great King Stag when Lion assailed him. There was no fight. The Great King's spirit left his body before Lion could touch him. It was a miracle.'

Looking past his father, Buckan could see that many eyes were now on him. Hundreds of stags stood in battle lines around the sloping escarpment. Behind the granite dome was the sheer drop to the river valley. Buckan knew that although the stags had control of the hill they could easily be pushed back over the edge of the cliff.

In front, beyond a small stream of spring water, hundreds of menacing wolf packs were snapping and snarling at them.

'They are waiting until the sun goes down,' said one of the stags. 'Then they will attack. They have been well organised, and tonight the full moon will heighten their savageness.'

'Heighten their fear, you mean. They seem uncertain. Where are the pack elders?' asked Buckan.

He turned towards the brave stags, and their expressions changed. They appeared resolute and stood taller as he looked into their eyes. His arrival seemed to have brought them strength. He must honour their faith with his own courage. Sensing a deep purpose, he was inspired to speak.

'Brave friends,' he cried, walking into the lines of stags. 'I bring a message from the Great King Stag. Be of clear and pure hearts as we fight to bring peace and freedom back to our land. Have faith. Before us, in the ranks of the wolves, lies delusion. They feed off one another's fear. Theirs is a sad and lonely world full of destruction. They cannot win, my brave friends, for they are lost. We shall hold fast on this sturdy rock. They will attack us, and we shall defend with our strong hearts. We will be tested to breaking point, but we shall prevail because the source of love is unlimited and our cause is just. My friends, we fight for love and valour.'

On hearing these words, the stags let out a loud battle cry: 'For love and valour!'

Perhaps it was not just his words that gave them strength. Perhaps they sensed another presence. For, as Buckan stood before them, he was also in Mountain Garden: there, the grass was vibrating at his hooves, light was engulfing him, and the waterfall resonated through him, bringing calm. In the twilight he saw the Great King Stag standing before him, surrounded by golden light.

CHAPTER XI

BATTLE

THE SUN WAS DESCENDING BEHIND THE wolves, casting deep shadows over the land. They started to howl as the searing white light gave way to a blood-red sky.

The rising moon seemed larger than usual. Buckan felt a cold breeze lifting the hair on his back. The stags were silent as he passed through their ranks. He could smell their nervous sweat and fear. Some had wavering eyes and others remained steadfast.

He walked to the highest point on the rock, aware that his white coat was reflecting the moon's light. The wolves fell silent as he turned to look down on them. Pausing, he studied the moon's magnificence. In the fleeting silence he could feel its timeless allure. It was a reassuring presence and, like a falling beech leaf, a connection to the infinite.

The moonstruck wolves recommenced their whining. He glanced at the squabbling packs, seeing the savage faces with their crazed eyes glinting like the innumerable stars. His flank shuddered. The moon was directly behind him now.

At first the wolves edged towards the tense stag lines. They surged forward, leaping the small stream that divided them, and smashed into the splintering wall of antler bone. They snapped at the stags' exposed skin, seizing them and dragging them to the ground.

The fallen stags' desperate shrieks shot through Buckan's ears. He felt their pain and tears filled his eyes. His body trembled. His heart pounded as he witnessed their courage. Meeting their anxious eyes with compassionate resolve, he knew that he was seeing himself, and that connecting to the source of love was more powerful than any action he could take or words he could utter. He stood firm in the moon's glow and breathed.

The stags turned to meet his gaze before they surged forward, heedless of their wounds. 'For love and valour!' they cried over the din, helping their fallen comrades, and beating back the wolves with their swiping antlers and strong hooves.

A beetle crossed the granite in front of Buckan. It

rummaged for food in the moonlight and then fell on its back, its legs flailing, before it righted itself and ran into a small tuft of grass.

The brave stags met wave after wave of attacking wolves, but they could not withstand their ferocity and were pushed back.

Sensing a rout, the wolves rushed forward. They clambered over the strewn bodies of wolves and stags. Tired stags could no longer help their fallen comrades. Cries were filling Buckan's ears, tearing his heart apart. Loyal stag warriors were fighting from the depths of their spirit.

'My Lord,' shouted one, 'the lines cannot hold!'

Forced to the edge of the treacherous cliff, the stags' defence was broken. Panic rippled through the lines. Disorientated stags were losing their footing and falling. Others continued fighting, unable to escape.

Buckan galloped through the fractured ranks. His body was filled with immense energy. He tossed the crying wolves high into the air, as if moving branches aside in the beech woods. The other stags rallied behind him, attacking the wolves, and forcing them to turn. Buckan raced onward, like an eagle diving through a cloud, and the wolves began to flee.

He stopped at the small stream, breathing heavily, and scrutinised a commotion at the far side of the rock. Why were the wolves scattering at the bottom of the hill as if from a hurricane?

Steinbock the Mountain King appeared through the shadows with hundreds of other proud Steinbocks charging behind in tight formation. They made a gallant sight in the moonlight, holding their heads high as if with disdain. They cantered up to Buckan, creating a fresh defence against the regrouping wolves.

'Brave Lord, I'm here to fight the wolves,' said Steinbock. 'Your courage on the mountain instilled in me a higher purpose. We must help each other. I offer my strongest Steinbocks to join you in battle.'

'My friend, you too have shown great courage in coming here this night. Your help is timely and gladly received. You have travelled far from your kingdom in the mountains and I welcome you in alliance. Let us stand together.'

The fierce wolves were racing forward once more, leaping the stream. They clashed with Steinbock's forces, taking great losses. Steinbock stood at the battlefront alongside the resurgent stags, shouting orders and encouragement to the combined forces of deer and Steinbocks, who were repelling each new attack. The ragged wolves were throwing themselves at the lines.

Standing again on the rock above them, Buckan noticed the wolves tire on seeing him.

His breath tightened. He looked about him, his heart pounding. What was it? He looked upwards, and saw a cloud billowing across the sky. Its darkness obscured the moon's glow, and spread a shadow across the battlefield. Sensing a silent presence in the dark, Buckan turned quickly to see Bat fluttering at his side.

'My Lord,' said Bat, 'I am here to assist you, and I have enlisted thousands of my brothers. Since our meeting I have changed. In deceiving others, I deceived myself and wasted my life – like a ghost, repeating the same meaningless actions. I am now flying higher and have come to atone for my misdeeds.'

As he spoke, a great cloud of bats descended on the wolves, attacking their eyes and biting their soft muzzles. Some wolves rolled on the ground and others fled the battlefield. Steinbock moved forward to counterattack but Buckan stopped him.

'Brave Steinbock, hold your lines. We cannot know what is yet to come.'

Then turning to Bat, he said, 'My friend, I thank you for your brave alliance. You are truly transformed. Let us unite and uphold the best in us both.'

With the sun emerging over the horizon, the bats began to rise up in the dawn sky, a magnificent cloud of fluttering silhouettes returning to their caves.

The wolves were now scattered. The stags and Steinbocks stopped to rest at the small stream.

But Buckan could not rest. He felt sickened, and was looking anxiously around. His body began quivering as a fresh foe approached. A large pride of lions from the grasslands was advancing fast towards them, attacking the wolves in their path.

CHAPTER XII

DARK FORCE

BUCKAN WATCHED AS THE LIONS APPROACHED. The bewildered wolves fled for their lives. When the lions neared the small stream, anxious stags and Steinbocks looked towards him.

'Those deluded by the dark will fall victim to the dark,' Buckan said. 'But my dear friends, those who find the light within have already won.'

A harrowing shriek pierced the air. Buckan's heart jumped, and he turned to see two stags drop lifeless to the ground. With a thunderous roar a huge battle-scarred lion leapt at him, his red mane flying.

Buckan reared to avoid Lion. Simultaneously a cold wind brushed against the hairs of his neck. Recognition dawned as he turned to face the coldness, his breath becoming stifled. Two piercing black eyes now gazed into his, and shadowy thunderclouds closed in upon his mind.

The serpent was uncoiling to her full height in

front of him. She swayed from side to side, flicking her tongue, mesmerising him, preparing to strike.

Her diamond-shaped head and black body glinted in the sunlight, revealing turquoise flashes from the surface of her exquisite scales. Her long graceful tail lashed the ground. She opened her sharp jaws, and venom and blood dripped from her fangs.

Lightning struck Mountain Garden. Serpent and Buckan were alone, surrounded by storm-swept trees. Serpent's dark eyes pinned him to the spot, while his heart raced in the swirling gale. He heard the soothing sound of the waterfall and felt its vibration. He saw a wild rose, and above the swaying trees a double rainbow glowed intensely like a bridge across time, back to his fawnhood.

Buckan was becoming detached, taking deep breaths. He felt Serpent's agony, her bitterness and loneliness. He could see her illusion of separation. She was in the beautiful garden but she could not see it. Her face was changing into multiple forms – she had moved away from the heart and had lost herself in delusion. Buckan was finally free of her.

Lion stepped between him and the fearsome Serpent.

Buckan had forgotten Lion's formidable presence – but he detected no malice in him now, only goodness and courage.

'Out of my way, Lion, you fool, and let me finish this,' lisped Serpent.

'You will not touch this white stag while I am here to stop you,' said Lion. 'You tricked me into killing the Great King Stag by playing on my foolish pride. In truth, I was no match at all for that noble King. You thought I would die in the attempt. The reason I am alive is that you underestimated the Great King Stag. He gave his life to save mine and to save the Kingdom from your tyranny. Killing me would have brought the revenge of the lions against the deer. He knew that if he let me live I would come to see my error.'

'Have you not feasted on fine venison?' said Serpent. 'Don't you want to be rid of those who challenge your power to rule over this world, to impose your divine will on these weaklings?'

'Divine will is not ours to impose,' said Lion, 'and that lie serves only your own greed and thirst for power.'

'Be very careful what you say to me,' said Serpent

with a sharp hiss, her tail searching for a hold on the ground, 'for we have an agreement, you and I – you'd better honour it!'

'Your lies and dark deceptions have divided us from our true friends the deer. You manipulated the wolves, creating false enemies of the deer and killing the wolf elders who opposed you. I would rather die than see you rule over this land with oppression.'

Turning towards Buckan, Lion said, 'Lord of the Deer, we met first at the clearing in the presence of the Great King Stag. I offer you the renewed alliance of the lions, as was the will of our ancestors.'

Serpent hissed and lashed out at Lion with lightning speed, sinking her fangs into his body. Lion then seized her with his strong jaws, biting off her head. Falling to the ground, Serpent's decapitated body whipped up dust clouds beside her. Buckan could see Lion's powerful body quivering as the deadly poison took hold.

'As I bit into the neck of the Great King Stag, I awoke from a nightmare. I resolved to foil Serpent's evil plans and on returning to the grasslands I instructed the lions to protect the deer. I hunted the huntress and she did not detect me, for she was preoccupied with you alone. I saw you pass her on a floating tree in the Dark Forest. This morning I saw her ascend the path behind us. I followed her. Perceiving her intention was to strike you down, my destiny was set.'

'Brave Lion,' said Buckan. 'You have fully redeemed your honour and I humbly accept our renewed alliance.'

On hearing these words Lion closed his flickering eyes, and was still.

Turning to the gathered deer and Steinbocks before him, his eyes misting over, Buckan spoke.

'The Great King Stag demonstrated immense wisdom and compassion in his every action. I now understand that by not fighting brave Lion he determined the outcome of the battle.'

The lion elders from the grasslands stepped towards Buckan, and Steinbock let them pass.

'We wish to honour our leader and affirm our allegiance to you, great Lord of the Deer. Let us never again take this alliance for granted, for freedom is easily eroded and evil quick to take its place. The wolves are now surrounded. What is to be done with them?'

'The very principles that Serpent sought to undermine will now save the wolves,' said Buckan. 'We can proceed with compassion and permit them to return safely to their homeland. Serpent's fearful power is vanquished. There is nothing to be gained from revenge. Let us forgive the wolves, and heal our differences, which are not so great. Let them be free.'

Buckan turned to address all in his presence, feeling Mountain Garden deep inside him.

'Within our hearts is a place of belonging. It is love that gives us strength. Let us deal kindly with each other, for though we come from different kingdoms we are connected by love.'

Epilogue

BUCKAN SOUGHT THE EXPANSE OF NATURE: the vibrant trees, the sound of the waterfall. He felt the beauty of each moment of existence. Peace enveloped him, a profound loving acceptance.

When he breathed the scent of the most exquisite spring blossoms, he sensed her closeness. Slipping beyond the shadows as the sun became a flaming disc at twilight, or in a glance through golden beech leaves in the autumn, or glimpsed out of the corner of his eye through a heavy snowstorm – he knew she was there.

One morning, a silhouette stepped through the rising dew: a beautifully tapered face with large celestial eyes reflecting the unveiling sky, the early spring sun picking out golden flecks on her slender body.

He recognised her as he gazed deep into the tender eyes of this golden doe and felt her love.

Grace was with him.

About the Author

Will Ottley grew up in rural Suffolk, England. He has travelled extensively and his experiences found expression in Mountain Garden, a book that he had always wanted to read. Will lives in London.

Printed in Great Britain
by Amazon